Seabird

Seabird

WRITTEN AND ILLUSTRATED BY

Holling Clancy Holling

A TRUMPET CLUB SPECIAL EDITION

Published by
The Trumpet Club
666 Fifth Avenue
New York, New York 10103

Copyright 1948 by Holling Clancy Holling
Copyright © renewed 1975 by Lucille Holling

The trademark Dell® is registered in the U.S. Patent and Trademark Office.
ISBN: 0-440-84115-1

Reprinted by arrangement with Houghton Mifflin Company
Printed in the United States of America
November 1989

10 9 8 7 6 5 4 3 2 1
UPC

TO

my friend

JACK BICKEL

— a young man of great promise —
who watched with helpful interest
the building of this book.

Acknowledgment

MANY friends helped with material for this book. They include librarian friends, who patiently provided armfuls of literature that I might prove for myself a point — no doubt unimportant; friends who loaned books, ship models, and technical advice when needed; museum friends, who dug through collections for articles to be studied and sketched; friends such as the forest ranger, who provided an opportunity for my clambering happily through a beached whale's skeleton; and three Pacific Coast Indians, who described for me the techniques and terrors of whale harpooning from canoes on the open sea. These friends include my long-suffering wife, riding convoy on SEABIRD with practiced hand and an eye for faulty steering; and my publisher who, waiting for SEABIRD to sail over successive deadlines, forwarded data and cheer above and beyond duty. To these helpers, the writer wishes to express his deepest gratitude.

Three books were especially useful in compiling information on whaling: THE YANKEE WHALER by Clifford W. Ashley ("the student, the artist, and the whaleman all in one") has the authentic grip of a barnacle on iron. . . . WHALESHIPS AND WHALING by Albert Cook Church is a source-book of rare photographs. Showing old whaleships and their men in intimate detail, some of the negatives were "actually rebuilt from broken bits of glass." . . . In GREASY LUCK, its author and illustrator, Gordon Grant, has re-created a strenuous activity in spirited pen sketches. Space does not permit the listing of all books consulted for technical data. However, any future whaleman, sailor, or armchair admiral can whet his salty appetite by cruising through the seagoing files of almost any library.

A writer of books for young people is quite aware that they may open new vistas for fresh and eager minds. If this story charts a course into related stories — sparkling seas now held unknown between other book covers — then SEABIRD will have accomplished part of her mission.

THE AUTHOR

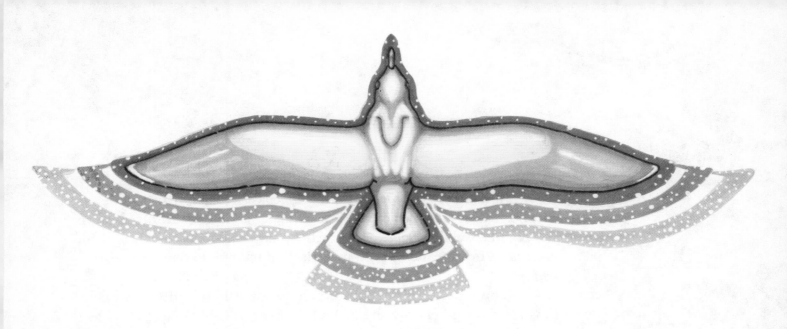

Contents

LARGE BIRDS, LEFT TO RIGH
GREAT BLACK-BACKED G
GLAUCOUS GU
HERRING GUL
IVORY GUL
ARCTIC TERM
AND BELOW,
RAVEN

1. THE IVORY GULL

SUMMER had come to the rocky coast of Greenland. The air throbbed with a clamor of seabirds calling. Glad cries tumbled down the sky like tinkling bells. They echoed until bald sea cliffs rang with chimes. Bird-screams swelled into blasts of trumpets above the beating surf.

Through all this happy tumult a snow-white bird flew silently. Smaller than other seagulls, it had their yellowish beak, but its feet were black. Its body and outstretched wings had no dark markings. The Ivory Gull looked like its name — a piece of carved ivory soaring in magic flight.

The flying Gull crossed frozen rivers of glaciers — gigantic icicles laid along the valleys. Moving inch by inch to the sea, they ended in ice walls towering up from the water. The land between these glaciers was wrinkled with hills. Long slopes shimmered with bright green, grassy fur. Hidden in grass, a Hare nibbled tops of dwarf trees stunted by Arctic cold. Through forests of flowers a white Fox stalked the Hare. But the Ivory Gull soared on.

Two mounds of snow by a brook turned into a Polar Bear and her cub catching trout with their paws. A greedy Raven hovered near-by in fitful circles. The black bird croaked at the white bird, but the Gull soared over and on without a sound.

Clouds of Arctic Terns swirled along the cliffs. Like large white Swallows they danced in the crisp, clear air. They seemed to call to the lonely Gull to join their play. But through all their swoops the Gull held its level flight.

It crossed an inlet walled by a sparkling glacier. An ice-chunk big as a hill split off from the walls and dropped into the sea. It sank and heaved upward again, a white mountain gushing foam. Thunders of its falling rolled for miles. Mad waves lashed the cliffs, rushed to sea tossing ice cakes, and lost themselves in the gray veil of a summer snowstorm. Yet even this birth of a floating iceberg had not caused the Ivory Gull to change its course. Somewhere northward its mate was waiting. It soared on and vanished in falling snow.

8

2. THE VISION IN THE SNOW

THE summer snowstorm not only blotted out the coast; it shut out sun, land, and sea. Caught in a tidal current, a whaling ship ran in this white haze like a blind thing being pushed.

The keen-eyed lad, high in the crow's-nest, was a worried lookout. Here he was, fourteen, a year out of New Bedford. For this whaling voyage he had signed on as the Ship's Boy. And now they trusted his searching eyes at the masthead. But how could anyone be expected to see dangerous rocks through this snow? He stamped his cold feet in the flimsy canvas barrel. Below him the mast melted into white nothing. Spars with furled sails made scarecrow arms. His lookout barrel seemed to float upward in a falling sky. . . . To Ezra Brown the world was all unreal. . . .

A shadow passed him, gone before he really saw it. It came again and was gone. Then it hovered, beyond arm's reach. A white bird soared motionless in the falling snow, looking at him. It gave no cry. It, too, was unreal to Ezra — as though the silent flakes had formed a snowy vision. The boy gazed without blinking. He had never seen anything so coldly beautiful — so much a part of snow and fog and the mystery of air. . . .

Without warning the white bird wheeled, swept forward and shot straight up. . . . It's gone, thought Ezra. Why did it go so fast? . . . As in a dream, he remembered a playful Swallow back home in Maine. It liked to fly toward a steep barn wall, then swoop upward, missing a crash by inches. And now this seabird — this Ivory Gull out of the Arctic — did the same thing. One minute it hung in the snow, and the next it swung out and up, like climbing a cliff ——

The memory snapped Ezra out of his trance as though struck by a harpoon. Even before he felt the blast of colder air on his face, he knew. He found his voice and bellowed into the white haze — 'ICE– BERG! ICEBERG! DEAD AHEAD!'

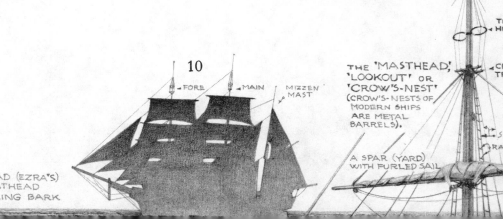

THE 'MASTHEAD,' 'LOOKOUT' OR 'CROW'S-NEST' (CROW'S-NESTS OF MODERN SHIPS ARE METAL BARRELS).

THE HOOP

CROSS TREES

SHRO

RATLIN

A SPAR (YARD) WITH FURLED SAIL

FORE ·MAIN · MIZZEN MAST

FORE MASTHEAD (EZRA'S) AND MAIN MASTHEAD ON THE WHALING BARK

3. SMART TRADERS

A HEAD-ON collision with an iceberg has sunk many a vessel. But at Ezra's wild yells the ship swerved away in time. It scraped the ice with a shudder that nearly shook the boy from his nest. Then the Whaler went on, unharmed.

The snowstorm passed swiftly. It seemed to Ezra that the Ivory Gull had swept it away — as though this snow-sprite, wrapped in a mystic veil, had vanished with it across the ice-flecked sea. . . .

When he climbed down to the deck, his tale of a 'bird that saved the ship' was twisted into different meanings by the crew. One, for instance, was afraid. 'Ez,' he groaned, ''twas a pale, white ghost you saw! Some lost, frozen whaleman's soul come out of the North a-flappin' — to haunt this ship!'

'He's sea-crazy!' laughed a Harpooner. ''Twas a *good* spirit, Ez, if spirit it was! 'Twill bring us plenty whale oil, this cruise!'

Ezra knew that his 'Seabird' was neither a ghost nor bad omen. He had seen many Ivory Gulls in Arctic waters. Yet this one, by flying off so oddly, had called his attention to the floating island of ice.

The Seabird might have remained with Ezra as only a memory, hovering in a halo of shining light. But one day while they were passing a rocky headland, an Eskimo's sealskin kayak put out, and raced to the ship with double paddle flashing.

This chuckling Eskimo knew how to trade with whalemen! Yes, indeed! He clambered up to the deck, hoisting a bale of furs behind him. Oh, what a smart trader he was! He grinned just right, he frowned just right, and he paddled away with a fortune! . . .

For a mere kayak-load of Fox and Polar Bear skins, the childish whalemen had given him genuine cotton cloth, a roll of it, and ten real iron fishhooks! Ah! And solid glass beads, too hard to dent with your teeth, yet with holes clear through them! But most priceless bargain of all — for two Walrus tusks, a boy had given him a little pump-drill of iron! With this magic thing you could make holes in wood or bone or ivory — rows and rows of holes! . . .

As for Ezra, those tusks and the Ivory Gull shaped his life.

12

WALRUS TUSKS RAKE CLAMS OUT OF SEA-BOTTOM. JAWS CHEW SHELLS AND ALL.

DRILLING IVORY WITH TWIRLED WALRUS WHISKER IS SLOW WORK.

A JIGGING PUMP-DRILL SPINS THIS WAY — THAT WAY — AND THROUGH IN A FEW SECONDS.

'STANDING RIGGING' BRACES MASTS FORE AND AFT. ▶ 'RUNNING RIGGING' (NOT SHOWN HERE) CHANGES SAIL ETC.

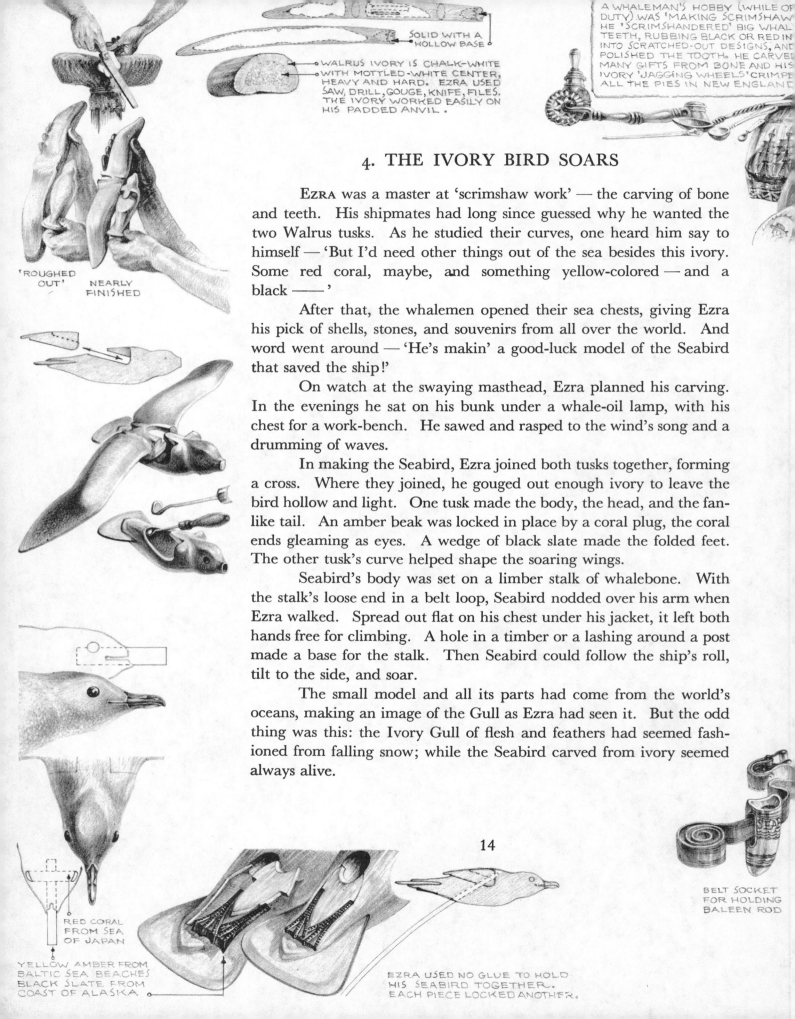

A WHALEMAN'S HOBBY (WHILE OF
DUTY) WAS 'MAKING SCRIMSHAW'
HE 'SCRIMSHANDERED' BIG WHAL
TEETH, RUBBING BLACK OR RED IN
INTO SCRATCHED-OUT DESIGNS, AND
POLISHED THE TOOTH. HE CARVED
MANY GIFTS FROM BONE AND HIS
IVORY 'JAGGING WHEELS' CRIMPE
ALL THE PIES IN NEW ENGLAND

SOLID WITH A
HOLLOW BASE

WALRUS IVORY IS CHALK-WHITE
WITH MOTTLED-WHITE CENTER,
HEAVY AND HARD. EZRA USED
SAW, DRILL, GOUGE, KNIFE, FILES.
THE IVORY WORKED EASILY ON
HIS PADDED ANVIL.

'ROUGHED
OUT'   NEARLY
FINISHED

4. THE IVORY BIRD SOARS

EZRA was a master at 'scrimshaw work' — the carving of bone and teeth. His shipmates had long since guessed why he wanted the two Walrus tusks. As he studied their curves, one heard him say to himself — 'But I'd need other things out of the sea besides this ivory. Some red coral, maybe, and something yellow-colored — and a black ——'

After that, the whalemen opened their sea chests, giving Ezra his pick of shells, stones, and souvenirs from all over the world. And word went around — 'He's makin' a good-luck model of the Seabird that saved the ship!'

On watch at the swaying masthead, Ezra planned his carving. In the evenings he sat on his bunk under a whale-oil lamp, with his chest for a work-bench. He sawed and rasped to the wind's song and a drumming of waves.

In making the Seabird, Ezra joined both tusks together, forming a cross. Where they joined, he gouged out enough ivory to leave the bird hollow and light. One tusk made the body, the head, and the fan-like tail. An amber beak was locked in place by a coral plug, the coral ends gleaming as eyes. A wedge of black slate made the folded feet. The other tusk's curve helped shape the soaring wings.

Seabird's body was set on a limber stalk of whalebone. With the stalk's loose end in a belt loop, Seabird nodded over his arm when Ezra walked. Spread out flat on his chest under his jacket, it left both hands free for climbing. A hole in a timber or a lashing around a post made a base for the stalk. Then Seabird could follow the ship's roll, tilt to the side, and soar.

The small model and all its parts had come from the world's oceans, making an image of the Gull as Ezra had seen it. But the odd thing was this: the Ivory Gull of flesh and feathers had seemed fashioned from falling snow; while the Seabird carved from ivory seemed always alive.

14

RED CORAL
FROM SEA
OF JAPAN

YELLOW AMBER FROM
BALTIC SEA BEACHES
BLACK SLATE FROM
COAST OF ALASKA

EZRA USED NO GLUE TO HOLD
HIS SEABIRD TOGETHER.
EACH PIECE LOCKED ANOTHER.

BELT SOCKET
FOR HOLDING
BALEEN ROD

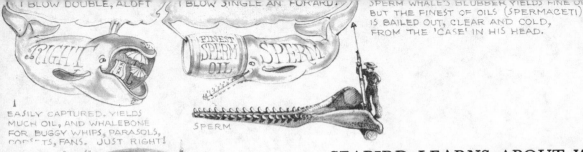

EASILY CAPTURED. YIELDS MUCH OIL, AND WHALEBONE FOR BUGGY WHIPS, PARASOLS, CORSETS, FANS. JUST RIGHT!

RIGHT HAS ODD BONY 'BONNET.'

BOWHEAD

HORNY WHALEBONE (BALEEN) IS LIGHT OR DARK, DEPENDING ON KIND OF WHALE. NOT BONE, IT SPLITS FINE ENOUGH TO MIX WITH SILK, MAKING SOME DRESSES RUSTLE.

MAINSTAYS OF OLD-TIME WHALING WERE SPERM, RIGHT AND BOWHEAD.

BOWHEAD LIKES ICY ARCTIC SEAS.

BONNET

RIGHT LIKES COLD WATERS.

SPERM PREFERS WARM SEAS.

A FEW COUSINS OF TOOTHED WHALES
HARBOR PORPOISE   BOTTLENOSE DOLPHIN   NARWHAL   KILLER

OLD WHALEMEN DISLIKED 'FINNERS' 'TOO FAST; SINK WHEN KILLED; BONE TOO SHORT;' TODAY, WHALEMEN TAKE THEM WITH SPEEDY MOTOR-CHASER BOATS AND HARPOON GUNS.

FINBACK WHALES

HUMPBACK FAIRLY FLIES.

FINBACK, SPEEDIEST WHALE.

BLUE (OR SULPHUR-BOTTOM) WHALE, LARGEST ANIMAL THAT EVER LIVED.

ABOVE ANIMALS TO SCALE: WEIGHT, ONE TON PER FOOT

5. SEABIRD LEARNS ABOUT WHALES

AND so the Seabird came to live with Ezra. Day after day while the ship worked southward, she soared beside him at the mast-head. One bright morning he cried, 'Look yonder, Seabird! That fountain of mist on the sea!' And cupping his hands, he called loudly, 'THAR SHE BLOWS! A RIGHT WHALE!'

'WHERE AWAY?' bawled the Skipper. 'LARBOARD BEAM! ONE MILE!' yelled Ezra.

Men scurried about on deck like startled chickens. Creaking ropes lowered three slender whaleboats. Long oars sped them away.

'Look at 'em go, Seabird!' laughed Ezra. 'We sure made 'em race for that Whale! But shucks, what do you know about Whales? They live in the sea, yet they aren't fish. They're animals, givin' milk to their young like cows. If they didn't "blow" at the surface an' take a new breath, they'd drown. All ——'

'HOW NOW?' called the Captain, and Ezra answered, 'WHALE ASLEEP ON THE SURFACE! WHALEBOATS RACIN' STEADY, THIRD MATE IN THE LEAD!

'All the Whales,' he continued, 'add up to just two kinds: those *with*, and those *without* teeth. Sperm Whales have teeth — big as over-sized cucumbers. They feed deep down along sea bottom, chompin' the wiggly tentacles of Giant Squid ——'

'WHERE NOW?' yelled the Skipper. Ezra squinted hard through a battered telescope before answering, 'ALMOST THERE!'

'Whales *without* teeth,' the boy went on, 'are Whalebone Whales — with stiff, springy curtains hangin' down in their mouths like giant feathers. Your teeterin' rod, Seabird, is made of this whalebone. Whaleboners, like that Right Whale they're chasin' now, eat shrimpy little creatures called "brit." The Whale plows the surface, mouth wide open, brit snags against his whalebone feathers; the water drains out, and old Whale gulps a bushel of brit at a time.'

'AIN'T THEY THERE *YET*?' bellowed the Captain.

'YES, SIR! GOIN' ON THE WHALE!' At those words, men swarmed into the rigging.

BOW BOAT, THIRD MATE, OFFICER

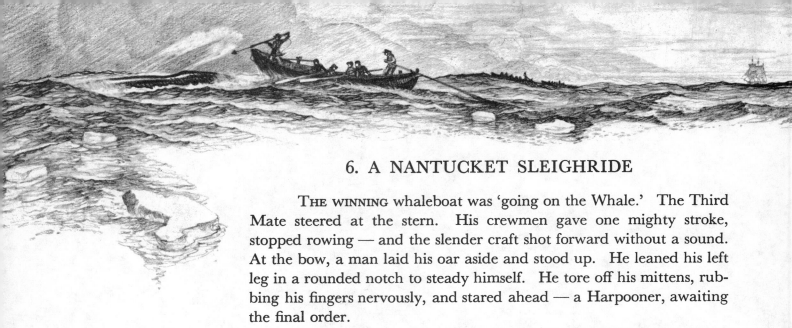

6. A NANTUCKET SLEIGHRIDE

THE WINNING whaleboat was 'going on the Whale.' The Third Mate steered at the stern. His crewmen gave one mighty stroke, stopped rowing — and the slender craft shot forward without a sound. At the bow, a man laid his oar aside and stood up. He leaned his left leg in a rounded notch to steady himself. He tore off his mittens, rubbing his fingers nervously, and stared ahead — a Harpooner, awaiting the final order.

The whaleboat drifted toward a dark bulk which wallowed in the swell like an overturned Schooner. Its back made a narrow island glistening in the sea.

'GIVE IT TO HIM!' yelped the Third Mate. The man at the bow swooped to the right, grabbed a harpoon from its rack, and heaved it straight at the shining island. He snatched a second harpoon and drove it overboard. Then he seemed to flee for his life.

He scrambled the length of the rocking whaleboat. Gaining the stern, he wrenched the steering oar from the Mate who lurched madly toward the bow. The two men seemed to be frantic people changing goals in a crazy game.

Then the Right Whale's huge tail flukes arose from the boiling sea. They towered like a giant's club — and crashed down. . . .

'Fuss an' foam!' cried Ezra, at the masthead. 'Seabird, those flukes *just* missed 'em! But heck! I'll bet your coral eyes can see better than this spyglass, even! You saw Harpooner get in both irons? An' Mate changin' places with him? Aye — a fool custom, that — changin' seats in a rockin' rowboat! But 'tis this way: one man spears the Whale, then steers; t'other steered the boat first, an' kills the Whale later with a long lance. Sort of evens up the dignity at both ends. . . .

'Look, Seabird! Whale's runnin' like a scairt colt across the sea, towin' the boat like a sled, with foamy suds for snow ——'

'WHAT NOW?' the Skipper bellowed from below. 'YOU ASLEEP UP THERE?'

'RUNAWAY!' yelled Ezra quickly. 'NANTUCKET SLEIGH-RIDE!'

18

CAPE ANN

BOSTON

CAPE COD

NEW BEDFORD AND NANTUCKET TWO OF THE OLDEST AND MOST FAMOUS WHALING PORTS IN AMERICA

THE 'HARPOONEER' (ONCE 'HARPOONIER' ~ SELDOM 'HARPOONER' TO OLD WHALEMEN) ~ THREW A 'HARPING IRON' WHICH CHANGED TO 'HARPOON' OR SIMPLY AN 'IRON'.

OLD-STYLE IRON IN USE WHEN SEABIRD WAS CARVED ~ 1830.

HICKORY 'POLE' WITH BARK ON

'TWO-FLUED' HEAD   SHANK   SOCKET

CHOCK PIN KEEPS LINE IN 'CHOCKS

LEG REST

'BOAT CROTCH' RACK

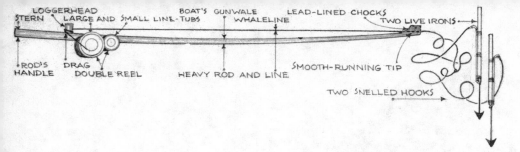

LOGGERHEAD
STERN · LARGE AND SMALL LINE-TUBS · BOAT'S GUNWALE · LEAD-LINED CHOCKS
WHALELINE · TWO LIVE IRONS
ROD'S HANDLE · DRAG DOUBLE-REEL · HEAVY ROD AND LINE · SMOOTH-RUNNING TIP
TWO SNELLED HOOKS

7. A GALLOPIN' FISHPOLE

'THIS WHALING must puzzle you a heap, Seabird,' said Ezra. 'But it's simple. That whaleboat out there is really a gallopin' fishpole. The pole's line is no thicker'n a thumb, an' floppy as an old shoelace, but it could hoist two wagonloads of hay an' not bust. It's coiled neat in one tub till that's full, then it loops over to fill another tub. Next it runs aft for a turn or two around the "loggerhead post" — an' then forward out a notch in the bow to the two harpoons. When the struck Whale runs, the whaleline fairly smokes around that loggerhead post. Men slosh it with sea water so it won't catch fire with the friction. They snub it tighter around the post till the boat gets under way without a jerk. When the Whale stops to rest, they haul in the line an' coil it again, like windin' up a fishline on a reel, you see. Then the rod an' the travelin' fishermen are all set for the next rush. This sort of thing can go on day an' night, sometimes. But when the beast is plumb tuckered, the boat-master leans over the gunnel an' finishes him off with a long lance.'

'COMIN' THIS WAY!' yelled someone. 'THEY'LL CRASH ON THAT FLOATIN' ICE!'

'NO, THEY WON'T!' bawled a loud voice. 'TH' MAN AT TH' STERN IS NOT ONLY A SMART *HARPOONER*, HE'S A MIGHTY SMART *BOAT STEERER*, TOO!'

The Whale's dash through a few ice cakes gave the Boat Steerer the chance of a lifetime to show off before the whole ship. He steered the craft in fancy swoops among jagged white islands. It danced through danger.

Ezra laid aside his telescope. He looked down on upturned faces in the craft speeding past. The shipboard audience roared and waved, and the whalemen answered. The Boat Steerer even took one hand from his oar to wave it wildly.

'DIDN'T I TELL YOU HE WAS A SMART ——' began the loud voice. Ezra heard a ripping crash. The whaleboat dissolved around one lonely ice cake. The end of the whaleline whipped from the shattered bow and sank in the sea.

20

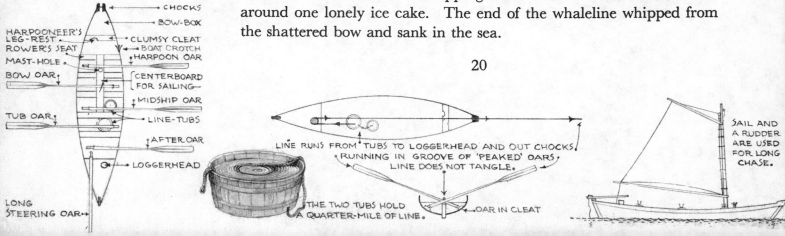

HARPOONEER'S LEG-REST · ROWER'S SEAT · MAST-HOLE · BOW OAR · TUB OAR · LONG STEERING OAR
CHOCKS · BOW-BOX · CLUMSY CLEAT · BOAT CROTCH · HARPOON OAR · CENTERBOARD FOR SAILING · MIDSHIP OAR · LINE-TUBS · AFTER OAR · LOGGERHEAD
LINE RUNS FROM TUBS TO LOGGERHEAD AND OUT CHOCKS, RUNNING IN GROOVE OF 'PEAKED' OARS, LINE DOES NOT TANGLE.
THE TWO TUBS HOLD A QUARTER-MILE OF LINE. · OAR IN CLEAT
SAIL AND A RUDDER ARE USED FOR LONG CHASE.

ANCIENT OIL LAMPS FROM EUROPE AND ASIA

→STONE
←CLAY
←BRONZE

SNUFFERS

TIN

PEWTER

GLASS

WHALE OIL LAMPS,
ANCESTORS OF
KEROSENE LAMPS

◄ TWELVE-FOOT LANCE WAS
THRUST (NOT THROWN)
TO KILL WHALE.

8. FIN OUT

'MEN OVERBOARD!' yelled the crew, then fell silent as the Captain cried, '*SMART*, WERE THEY? I'LL SMART 'EM!'

A boat was lowered and sped toward the men clinging to oars and tubs. That water was cold! Ezra shivered. The Seabird tilted, touching his cap with a wing tip. 'Yep, I know what you're sayin' — Skipper's mad, an' we're lucky not to be near him. But look! Whale's runnin' blind-like between the other two boats! Can they — yep! BOTH BOATS STRUCK THE WHALE! HE'S SOUNDING!'

The crew raced for the rigging again, the Captain with them. He said nothing when the six half-drowned men returned.

Ezra watched the distant boats, waiting for the Whale to come up. He also watched the Captain below him. The Old Man climbed slowly, pausing now and then to gaze thoughtfully out to sea. After what seemed ages, he reached the masthead.

'Whale's been down a half-hour,' he said. 'Tired an' sore wounded. I say he'll breach surface in twenty minutes. What say you, Boy?'

'W-well, Sir,' stammered Ezra. 'I'd have said five.'

'Disagree with me, eh? Want to bet? If your *five* minutes wins, ye'll have supper some night with me in my cabin. Does the Whale breach nearer *twenty* minutes, ye'll stand extra watch for a week. Mind, ye don't have to take the bet!'

'I'll take it, Sir,' said Ezra. The Captain looked at his watch.

The boy clung to his wobbling telescope. He felt like a fool for daring to wager with the Old Man! . . . He sweated. . . . He squirmed. . . . Years seemed to roll over him. . . . He saw spots — or was it a Whale against the sky?

'BREACHIN'!' he shrieked. 'B-beg pardon, Sir — he's come up!'

'Aye,' said the Skipper, watching the soaring Seabird and almost smiling. 'And his flukes are lashin' the sea to foam with his fury. But not for long. He's played out. They'll lance him soon — tiny men will kill a mighty Whale, an' he'll die on his side, fin out of water. . . . Let's see. Five — six minutes it was. Ye win, fair. A supper . . . LOOK ALIVE BELOW! HELP TOW IN THAT WHALE!'

'AYE'
PRONOUN
LIKE LO
MEANS '

A 'SOUNDING' WHALE
MAY DIVE A MILE IN A
FEW MINUTES. 'BREACHING'
HE MAY RISE SLOWLY, OR LEAP
OUT OF WATER. SPERM WHALES HAVE
SUNK WHALING SHIPS BY SUCH CHARGES.

AFTER BEING LANCED, A WHALE
'GOES INTO A FLURRY' WITH
LASHING FLUKES. 'FIN OUT'
MEANS 'DEAD

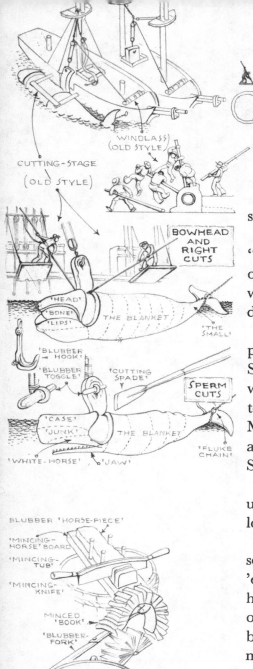

9. CUTTING IN

THE SEABIRD soared at the masthead in a cloud of greasy black smoke.

'No, the ship's not afire,' coughed Ezra beside her. 'That's the "try-works" on deck, heatin' two big iron kettles, boilin' whale oil out of blubber. Why? So that candles an' whale-oil lamps can light the world. Funny, isn't it — bright lamplight fished up from the cold, dark depths of the sea!

'Look! The dead Whale floats alongside our ship. They're peelin' him in one long strip, wide as a man is tall, an' thick as his body. See, they slip a huge iron hook through a hole in the hide. Hear the windlass squealin' as the tackle hoists the hook! Over we go — tipped toward the Whale by the strain of pulling. Now look straight down. Men are pokin' the white blubber loose with sharp irons like oars. In a second, ten more feet of hide will come away sudden — hold tight, Seabird!' Ezra clung to the mast while Seabird circled madly.

'You'll get used to it,' laughed the boy. 'This cuttin' in is like unrollin' a heavy carpet. The carcass flops over as the hide comes loose, an' rocks the ship.

'A greasy mess it is, choppin' up that hide for the try-pots. Big squares first, then fencepost sizes, then long loaves of bread. Watch 'em cuttin' these down to the skin — like leavin' thick bread-slices hangin' to a leathery bottom crust. The white blubber melts into whale oil in the kettles. But the skin pieces bob around like twisted strips of bacon rind. They fish that out an' toss the chunks into the fire. It makes hot flames an' all this sooty smoke.

'Yep, Seabird — in the middle of an ocean, far from wood or coal, a Whale's hide boils out its own oil. . . . But they'll *boil me* if I don't get below an' help. You stay up here an' keep your coral eyes open!'

Clouds of squalling Gulls circled the ship, puzzled by a smaller Gull which clung to one of the masts. The silent Seabird soared aloof while the others dove for scraps around the derelict Whale.

24

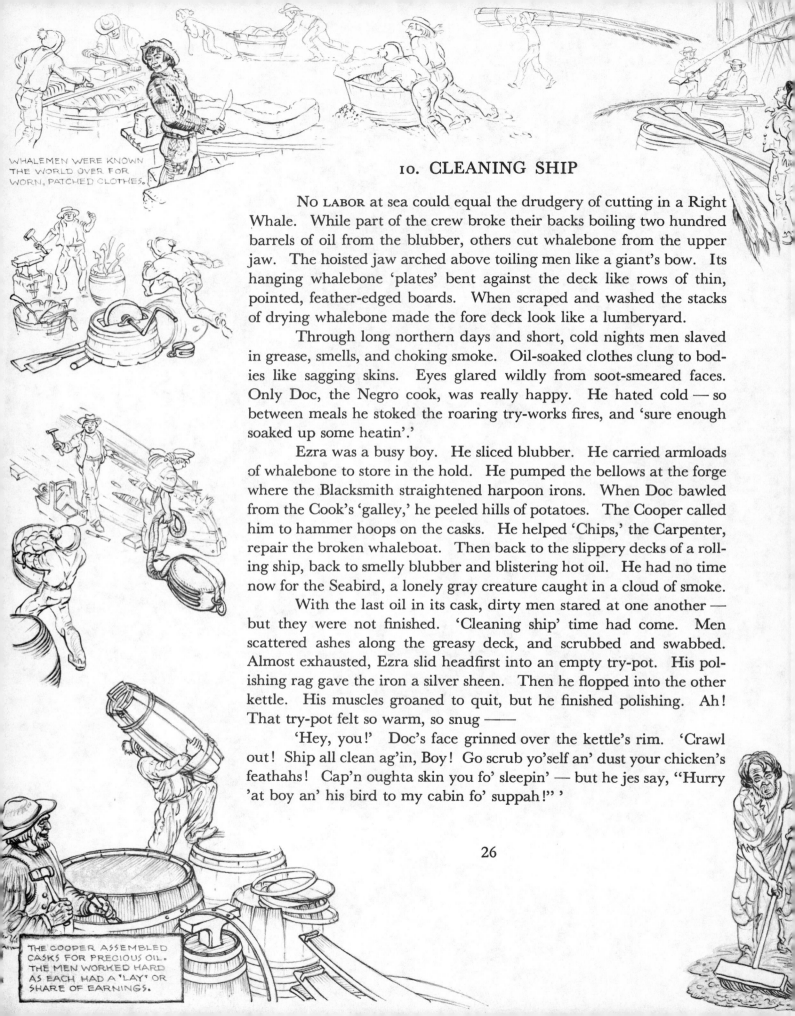

WHALEMEN WERE KNOWN
THE WORLD OVER FOR
WORN, PATCHED CLOTHES.

10. CLEANING SHIP

No LABOR at sea could equal the drudgery of cutting in a Right Whale. While part of the crew broke their backs boiling two hundred barrels of oil from the blubber, others cut whalebone from the upper jaw. The hoisted jaw arched above toiling men like a giant's bow. Its hanging whalebone 'plates' bent against the deck like rows of thin, pointed, feather-edged boards. When scraped and washed the stacks of drying whalebone made the fore deck look like a lumberyard.

Through long northern days and short, cold nights men slaved in grease, smells, and choking smoke. Oil-soaked clothes clung to bodies like sagging skins. Eyes glared wildly from soot-smeared faces. Only Doc, the Negro cook, was really happy. He hated cold — so between meals he stoked the roaring try-works fires, and 'sure enough soaked up some heatin'.'

Ezra was a busy boy. He sliced blubber. He carried armloads of whalebone to store in the hold. He pumped the bellows at the forge where the Blacksmith straightened harpoon irons. When Doc bawled from the Cook's 'galley,' he peeled hills of potatoes. The Cooper called him to hammer hoops on the casks. He helped 'Chips,' the Carpenter, repair the broken whaleboat. Then back to the slippery decks of a rolling ship, back to smelly blubber and blistering hot oil. He had no time now for the Seabird, a lonely gray creature caught in a cloud of smoke.

With the last oil in its cask, dirty men stared at one another — but they were not finished. 'Cleaning ship' time had come. Men scattered ashes along the greasy deck, and scrubbed and swabbed. Almost exhausted, Ezra slid headfirst into an empty try-pot. His polishing rag gave the iron a silver sheen. Then he flopped into the other kettle. His muscles groaned to quit, but he finished polishing. Ah! That try-pot felt so warm, so snug ——

'Hey, you!' Doc's face grinned over the kettle's rim. 'Crawl out! Ship all clean ag'in, Boy! Go scrub yo'self an' dust your chicken's feathahs! Cap'n oughta skin you fo' sleepin' — but he jes say, "Hurry 'at boy an' his bird to my cabin fo' suppah!"'

26

THE COOPER ASSEMBLED
CASKS FOR PRECIOUS OIL.
THE MEN WORKED HARD
AS EACH HAD A 'LAY' OR
SHARE OF EARNINGS.

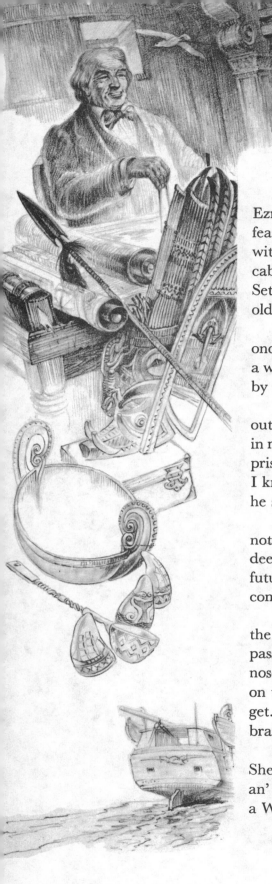

11. IN THE CAPTAIN'S CABIN

THAT EVENING, Doc served a spicy meal right out of the Orient. Ezra felt like the guest of a King as the Captain taught him to eat this feast with chopsticks. After supper they entered a small room crowded with ship models, instruments, charts, trinkets, and books. 'Here's my cabin,' Skipper was saying, 'hangin' over the rudder like a balcony. Set Seabird to look out the ports, as I do, at the wake of the ship. An old man, ye see, spends much time lookin' back at the past. . . .

'Aye, lookin' back. . . . Ye might never think it, Ezra, but I was once a boy; and I had a toy bird. My father brought it from China -- a white paper thing. Soft feathers it had, and gilded eyes. And it held by its beak to a string. And it soared in the wind. . . .

'Such toys can work magic. Mine did. From a cliff it sailed out like a tiny kite, high above surf. It twitched an' tugged at the line in my hand — coaxin' me out with it, off across the seas. So 'tis not surprisin' that later I shipped as a sailor, an' climbed to be Captain. And I know that a boy who can carve the Seabird can be a Captain, too, if he sets his mind to it. . . .

'But you won't skipper a Whaler. Why? Well, whale oil will not always light the world. 'Twill give way to oil pumped up from deep in the earth. Some big cities already have gaslight. But, be the future lamps lit by earth-oil, gas, or even lightning itself — the day will come when Whalers will no more put to sea. . . .

'At times I wonder why I stuck to Whalers. They're known to the world as "Slaughterhouses" and "Stinkers!" When a prim ship passes to leeward, dainty passengers at the rail clap kerchiefs to their noses! 'Tis a strange feelin' to recollect that your ship lays a foul odor on the breeze. Livin' so long with smells of blood an' blubber, ye forget. Ye feel hurt for your vessel — a soiled child that stiff-starched brats won't play with! . . .

'Aye — a Whaler's a dirty tub! Yet no ship has more dignity! She takes fair weather or foul; licks her own wounds on the open sea; an' doesn't run home till her casks are full, if it takes four years. . . . Ez, a Whaler's Cap'n can teach things, if ye wish to learn.'

28

FOC'S'L
(FORE-CAST
HATCH
TO THE C
QUARTE

FORE
HATCH

DOWN
TO
OFFICERS'
QUARTERS
AND
CAPTAIN'S
CABIN

COOK
GALL

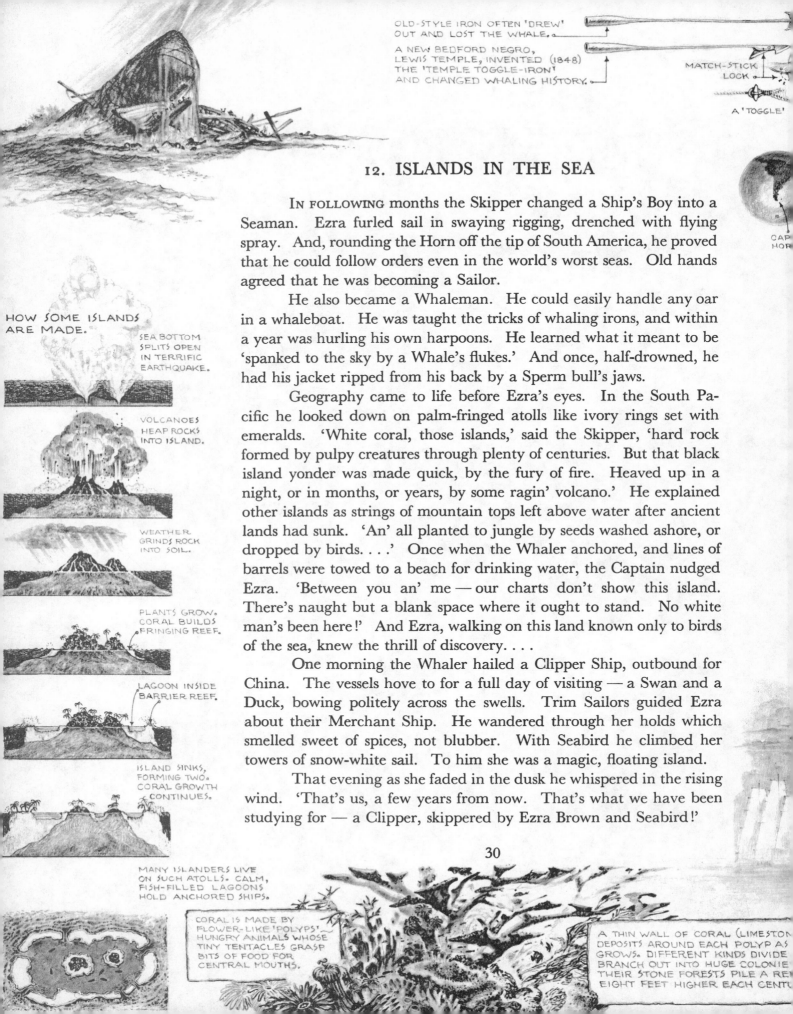

OLD-STYLE IRON OFTEN 'DREW' OUT AND LOST THE WHALE.

A NEW BEDFORD NEGRO, LEWIS TEMPLE, INVENTED (1848) THE 'TEMPLE TOGGLE-IRON' AND CHANGED WHALING HISTORY.

MATCH-STICK LOCK

A 'TOGGLE'

CAPE HORN

12. ISLANDS IN THE SEA

IN FOLLOWING months the Skipper changed a Ship's Boy into a Seaman. Ezra furled sail in swaying rigging, drenched with flying spray. And, rounding the Horn off the tip of South America, he proved that he could follow orders even in the world's worst seas. Old hands agreed that he was becoming a Sailor.

He also became a Whaleman. He could easily handle any oar in a whaleboat. He was taught the tricks of whaling irons, and within a year was hurling his own harpoons. He learned what it meant to be 'spanked to the sky by a Whale's flukes.' And once, half-drowned, he had his jacket ripped from his back by a Sperm bull's jaws.

Geography came to life before Ezra's eyes. In the South Pacific he looked down on palm-fringed atolls like ivory rings set with emeralds. 'White coral, those islands,' said the Skipper, 'hard rock formed by pulpy creatures through plenty of centuries. But that black island yonder was made quick, by the fury of fire. Heaved up in a night, or in months, or years, by some ragin' volcano.' He explained other islands as strings of mountain tops left above water after ancient lands had sunk. 'An' all planted to jungle by seeds washed ashore, or dropped by birds. . . .' Once when the Whaler anchored, and lines of barrels were towed to a beach for drinking water, the Captain nudged Ezra. 'Between you an' me — our charts don't show this island. There's naught but a blank space where it ought to stand. No white man's been here!' And Ezra, walking on this land known only to birds of the sea, knew the thrill of discovery. . . .

One morning the Whaler hailed a Clipper Ship, outbound for China. The vessels hove to for a full day of visiting — a Swan and a Duck, bowing politely across the swells. Trim Sailors guided Ezra about their Merchant Ship. He wandered through her holds which smelled sweet of spices, not blubber. With Seabird he climbed her towers of snow-white sail. To him she was a magic, floating island.

That evening as she faded in the dusk he whispered in the rising wind. 'That's us, a few years from now. That's what we have been studying for — a Clipper, skippered by Ezra Brown and Seabird!'

30

HOW SOME ISLANDS ARE MADE.

SEA BOTTOM SPLITS OPEN IN TERRIFIC EARTHQUAKE.

VOLCANOES HEAP ROCKS INTO ISLAND.

WEATHER GRINDS ROCK INTO SOIL.

PLANTS GROW. CORAL BUILDS FRINGING REEF.

LAGOON INSIDE BARRIER REEF.

ISLAND SINKS, FORMING TWO. CORAL GROWTH CONTINUES.

MANY ISLANDERS LIVE ON SUCH ATOLLS. CALM, FISH-FILLED LAGOONS HOLD ANCHORED SHIPS.

CORAL IS MADE BY FLOWER-LIKE 'POLYPS'— HUNGRY ANIMALS WHOSE TINY TENTACLES GRASP BITS OF FOOD FOR CENTRAL MOUTHS.

A THIN WALL OF CORAL (LIMESTONE) DEPOSITS AROUND EACH POLYP AS GROWS. DIFFERENT KINDS DIVIDE BRANCH OUT INTO HUGE COLONIE THEIR STONE FORESTS PILE A RE EIGHT FEET HIGHER EACH CENTU

13. THE CHANGING YEARS

To Seabird there was no such thing as time. In her ivory head, 'today' could be 'yesterday' or 'tomorrow,' and she was just as happy. She tilted, dipped, and soared according to the winds that blew. She was forever flying away, yet never left her base.

Her coral eyes had looked at many changes since her birth and first voyage on the Whaler. Ezra's friend the Skipper had taught him well. Ezra finished each ship-school task with the same care he had put into carving the Seabird. He rose to be First Mate, and at last held a Master's papers. Owners of merchant vessels tried him out on their toughest hulks, for they had a later surprise in store for him. They found that Captain Ezra Brown had a way with ships and with those who manned them. He yelled only to lift his voice above the roar of wind; otherwise he talked in low, clear tones — and men obeyed him.

Meanwhile Ezra had married a girl with golden hair and eyes blue as the sea. One day he sailed home to find that he had a son, named Nathaniel. The whaling Skipper, too old now for sailing, came often 'to train Ezra's boy.' Thus 'Nate' could swim in a pond before he could walk — 'like any South Sea native!' And a few years later, Skipper had him diving from a high pier. 'But he's only a little *child*!' cried his worried mother, hurrying down to the beach.

Across an inlet, Nate stood atop some tall piling — a small, tanned figure with copper-red hair. 'See me! See me *now*!' he called over the water, swooping out and down. It seemed ages till he splashed, ages more before his red head bobbed above waves. As he laughed and swam shoreward, Skipper said, 'Look at 'im! Part monkey, part fish, part seagull! Your darlin' Nate may get into a heap of trouble, Ma'm — but you'll never have to worry when he's around water!'

Nate grew up wanting to fly like the Seabird. At first she had soared above his cradle, always hovering there when he awoke. He tried to get at her, but they kept her as hard to reach as a star. Not until he was ten did Ezra allow him to carry Seabird on his arm, as reward for good behavior. And this was the year that Nate, his father Ezra, and Seabird started voyaging together.

BARNACLES STICK TO ANY-THING AFLOAT~ EXCEPT COPPER-SHEATHED SHIPS. MODERN SHIPS OF STEEL CAN PICK UP THIRTY TONS OF THESE ANIMALS IN ONE YEAR, AND MUST HAVE THEIR HULLS SCRAPED. BUT WHALERS AND THE CLIPPERS WORE COPPER.

SHELL ABOUT FULL SIZE

MOUTHS

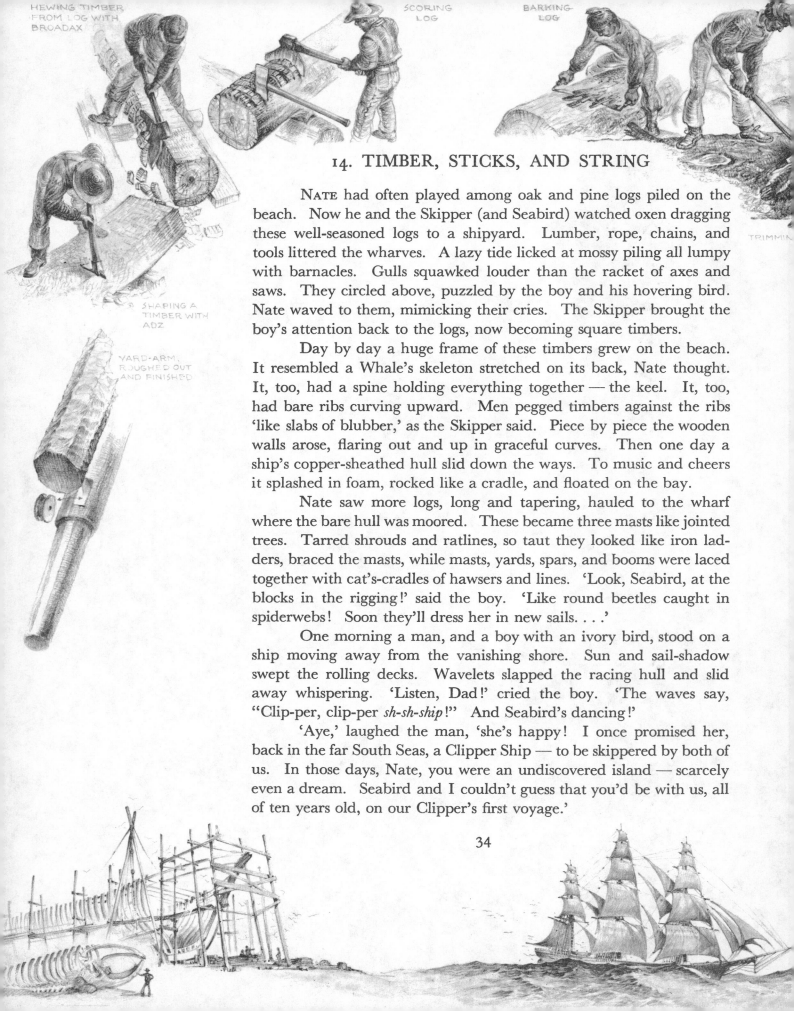

SHAPING A TIMBER WITH ADZ

YARD-ARM, ROUGHED OUT AND FINISHED

14. TIMBER, STICKS, AND STRING

NATE had often played among oak and pine logs piled on the beach. Now he and the Skipper (and Seabird) watched oxen dragging these well-seasoned logs to a shipyard. Lumber, rope, chains, and tools littered the wharves. A lazy tide licked at mossy piling all lumpy with barnacles. Gulls squawked louder than the racket of axes and saws. They circled above, puzzled by the boy and his hovering bird. Nate waved to them, mimicking their cries. The Skipper brought the boy's attention back to the logs, now becoming square timbers.

Day by day a huge frame of these timbers grew on the beach. It resembled a Whale's skeleton stretched on its back, Nate thought. It, too, had a spine holding everything together — the keel. It, too, had bare ribs curving upward. Men pegged timbers against the ribs 'like slabs of blubber,' as the Skipper said. Piece by piece the wooden walls arose, flaring out and up in graceful curves. Then one day a ship's copper-sheathed hull slid down the ways. To music and cheers it splashed in foam, rocked like a cradle, and floated on the bay.

Nate saw more logs, long and tapering, hauled to the wharf where the bare hull was moored. These became three masts like jointed trees. Tarred shrouds and ratlines, so taut they looked like iron ladders, braced the masts, while masts, yards, spars, and booms were laced together with cat's-cradles of hawsers and lines. 'Look, Seabird, at the blocks in the rigging!' said the boy. 'Like round beetles caught in spiderwebs! Soon they'll dress her in new sails. . . .'

One morning a man, and a boy with an ivory bird, stood on a ship moving away from the vanishing shore. Sun and sail-shadow swept the rolling decks. Wavelets slapped the racing hull and slid away whispering. 'Listen, Dad!' cried the boy. 'The waves say, "Clip-per, clip-per *sh-sh-ship*!" And Seabird's dancing!'

'Aye,' laughed the man, 'she's happy! I once promised her, back in the far South Seas, a Clipper Ship — to be skippered by both of us. In those days, Nate, you were an undiscovered island — scarcely even a dream. Seabird and I couldn't guess that you'd be with us, all of ten years old, on our Clipper's first voyage.'

34

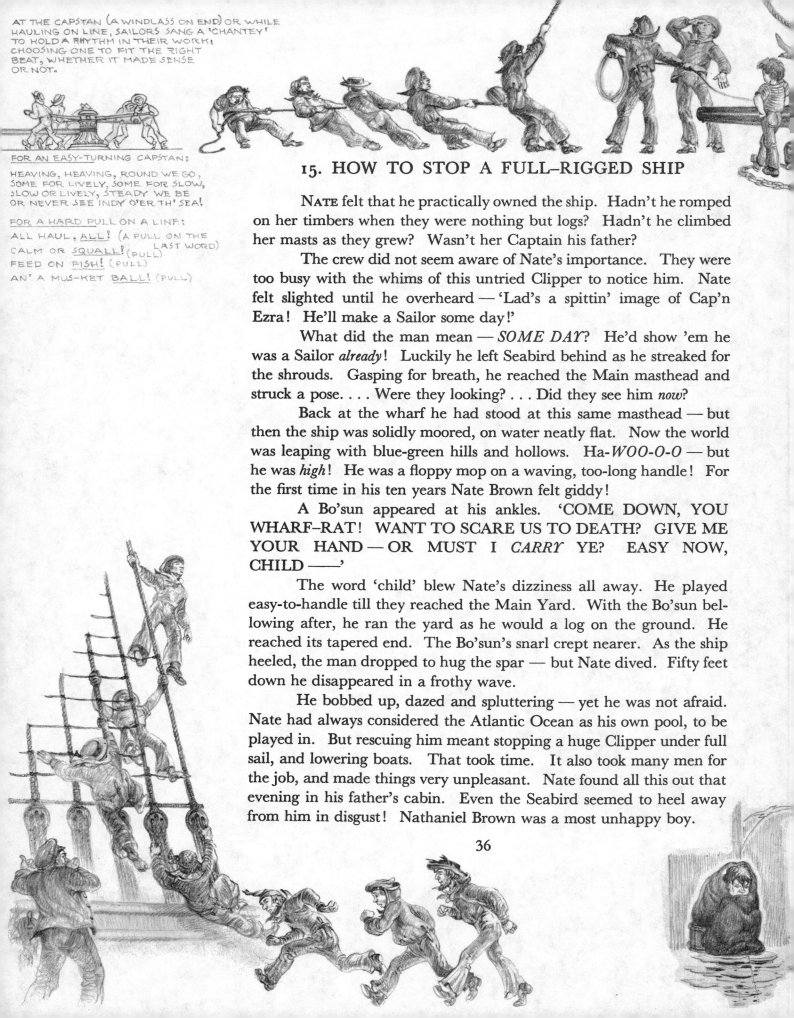

AT THE CAPSTAN (A WINDLASS ON END) OR WHILE
HAULING ON LINE, SAILORS SANG A 'CHANTEY'
TO HOLD A RHYTHM IN THEIR WORK,
CHOOSING ONE TO FIT THE RIGHT
BEAT, WHETHER IT MADE SENSE
OR NOT.

FOR AN EASY-TURNING CAPSTAN:

HEAVING, HEAVING, ROUND WE GO,
SOME FOR LIVELY, SOME FOR SLOW,
SLOW OR LIVELY, STEADY WE BE
OR NEVER SEE INDY O'ER TH' SEA!

FOR A HARD PULL ON A LINE:
ALL HAUL, ALL! (A PULL ON THE
CALM OR SQUALL! (PULL) LAST WORD)
FEED ON FISH! (PULL)
AN' A MUS-KET BALL! (PULL)

15. HOW TO STOP A FULL-RIGGED SHIP

NATE felt that he practically owned the ship. Hadn't he romped on her timbers when they were nothing but logs? Hadn't he climbed her masts as they grew? Wasn't her Captain his father?

The crew did not seem aware of Nate's importance. They were too busy with the whims of this untried Clipper to notice him. Nate felt slighted until he overheard — 'Lad's a spittin' image of Cap'n Ezra! He'll make a Sailor some day!'

What did the man mean — *SOME DAY*? He'd show 'em he was a Sailor *already*! Luckily he left Seabird behind as he streaked for the shrouds. Gasping for breath, he reached the Main masthead and struck a pose. . . . Were they looking? . . . Did they see him *now*?

Back at the wharf he had stood at this same masthead — but then the ship was solidly moored, on water neatly flat. Now the world was leaping with blue-green hills and hollows. Ha-*WOO-O-O* — but he was *high*! He was a floppy mop on a waving, too-long handle! For the first time in his ten years Nate Brown felt giddy!

A Bo'sun appeared at his ankles. 'COME DOWN, YOU WHARF-RAT! WANT TO SCARE US TO DEATH? GIVE ME YOUR HAND — OR MUST I *CARRY* YE? EASY NOW, CHILD ——'

The word 'child' blew Nate's dizziness all away. He played easy-to-handle till they reached the Main Yard. With the Bo'sun bellowing after, he ran the yard as he would a log on the ground. He reached its tapered end. The Bo'sun's snarl crept nearer. As the ship heeled, the man dropped to hug the spar — but Nate dived. Fifty feet down he disappeared in a frothy wave.

He bobbed up, dazed and spluttering — yet he was not afraid. Nate had always considered the Atlantic Ocean as his own pool, to be played in. But rescuing him meant stopping a huge Clipper under full sail, and lowering boats. That took time. It also took many men for the job, and made things very unpleasant. Nate found all this out that evening in his father's cabin. Even the Seabird seemed to heel away from him in disgust! Nathaniel Brown was a most unhappy boy.

36

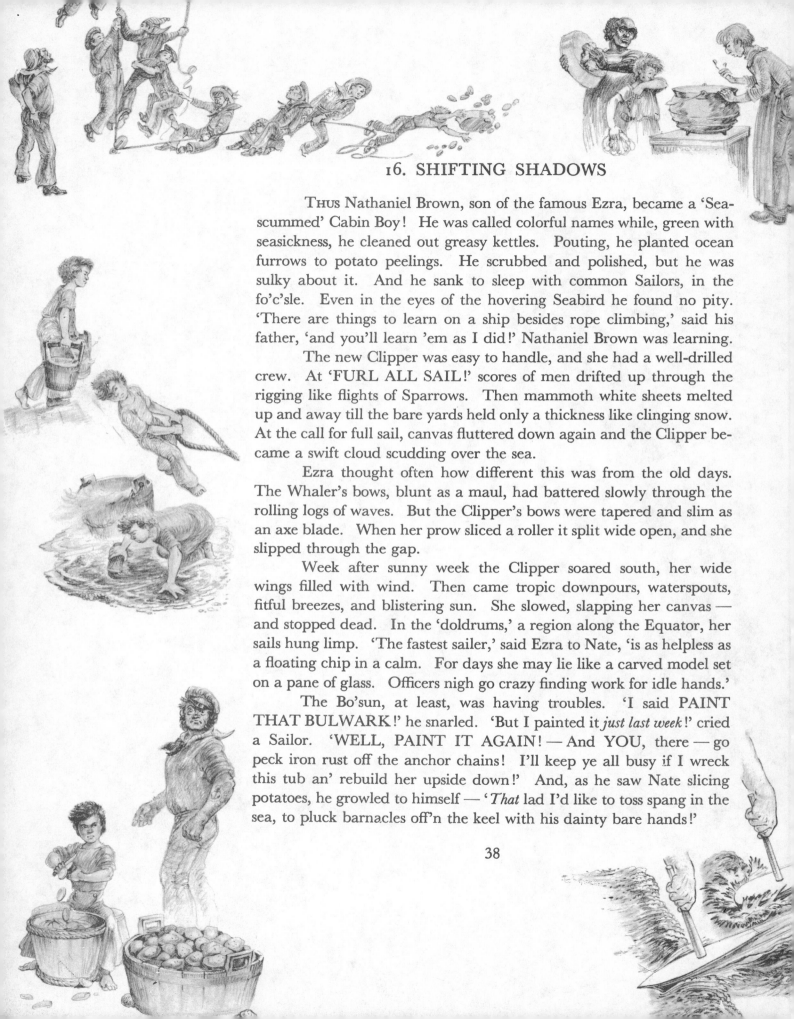

16. SHIFTING SHADOWS

THUS Nathaniel Brown, son of the famous Ezra, became a 'Sea-scummed' Cabin Boy! He was called colorful names while, green with seasickness, he cleaned out greasy kettles. Pouting, he planted ocean furrows to potato peelings. He scrubbed and polished, but he was sulky about it. And he sank to sleep with common Sailors, in the fo'c'sle. Even in the eyes of the hovering Seabird he found no pity. 'There are things to learn on a ship besides rope climbing,' said his father, 'and you'll learn 'em as I did!' Nathaniel Brown was learning.

The new Clipper was easy to handle, and she had a well-drilled crew. At 'FURL ALL SAIL!' scores of men drifted up through the rigging like flights of Sparrows. Then mammoth white sheets melted up and away till the bare yards held only a thickness like clinging snow. At the call for full sail, canvas fluttered down again and the Clipper became a swift cloud scudding over the sea.

Ezra thought often how different this was from the old days. The Whaler's bows, blunt as a maul, had battered slowly through the rolling logs of waves. But the Clipper's bows were tapered and slim as an axe blade. When her prow sliced a roller it split wide open, and she slipped through the gap.

Week after sunny week the Clipper soared south, her wide wings filled with wind. Then came tropic downpours, waterspouts, fitful breezes, and blistering sun. She slowed, slapping her canvas — and stopped dead. In the 'doldrums,' a region along the Equator, her sails hung limp. 'The fastest sailer,' said Ezra to Nate, 'is as helpless as a floating chip in a calm. For days she may lie like a carved model set on a pane of glass. Officers nigh go crazy finding work for idle hands.'

The Bo'sun, at least, was having troubles. 'I said PAINT THAT BULWARK!' he snarled. 'But I painted it *just last week*!' cried a Sailor. 'WELL, PAINT IT AGAIN! — And YOU, there — go peck iron rust off the anchor chains! I'll keep ye all busy if I wreck this tub an' rebuild her upside down!' And, as he saw Nate slicing potatoes, he growled to himself — '*That* lad I'd like to toss spang in the sea, to pluck barnacles off'n the keel with his dainty bare hands!'

38

17. LINES, WINDS, AND WAVES

On the day the Clipper reached the Equator, Captain Ezra suddenly dashed to the side. 'KING NEPTUNE!' he cried. 'WEL–COME ABOARD!' A man slopped over the rail in wet sacking, rope locks and whiskers. Tilting his tin pan crown and waving a fish spear, he bawled, 'ANY LUBBERS HERE WHO HAIN'T CROSSED THE LINE?' One helper hugged a huge wooden 'razor.' A silent man in a seaweed mask whirled a 'shaving brush' above a tub of tar.

With a dozen 'lubbers,' Nate was led to a chalk-line on deck. On this 'Equator' his jaws were tarred and 'shaved,' and he was soused in sea water. He had 'crossed the Line!' He capered with the others. He also bumped blindly into the man leaning over his tub of tar.

The crew roared with laughter. The man crawled from the tub, scooping gooey blackness from mouth and eyes. 'THAT WHARF–RAT! DONE IT A–PURPOSE! SHOWIN' OFF AG'IN!' he sputtered. The Bo'sun would never believe it was accidental.

South of the Line came more doldrums; then steady winds; then roaring gales; and then — THE HORN! Ezra called his son aft.

'Nate,' he said, 'your berth is in my cabin while we turn the corner of South America. I don't want you swimming off in *these* seas! Keep clear of wind *and* working Sailors. As to questions — ask Sea-bird. She's been here before!'

Gone now was the Clipper's gay trick of slicing waves. Water mountains crashed down upon her. Sails split with a roar. Spars snapped and carried away. Day after night after day the ship seemed haunted and terror-stricken; while half-dead Seamen fought for her life with sticks, string, and frozen cloth against the shrieking sky.

The Bo'sun seemed to be everywhere at once, relishing danger. He grinned in the very teeth of the howling gales. One day he knocked a sick Sailor downstairs with one blow. 'DON'T *NOBODY* TRY TO PLAY SICK WITH *ME*!' he bawled, still grinning.

A weary Mate shook his head when he heard about it. 'Bo'sun takes fire too easy! But so far nobody's gone overboard. If this Clip-per's good luck can last ——'

40

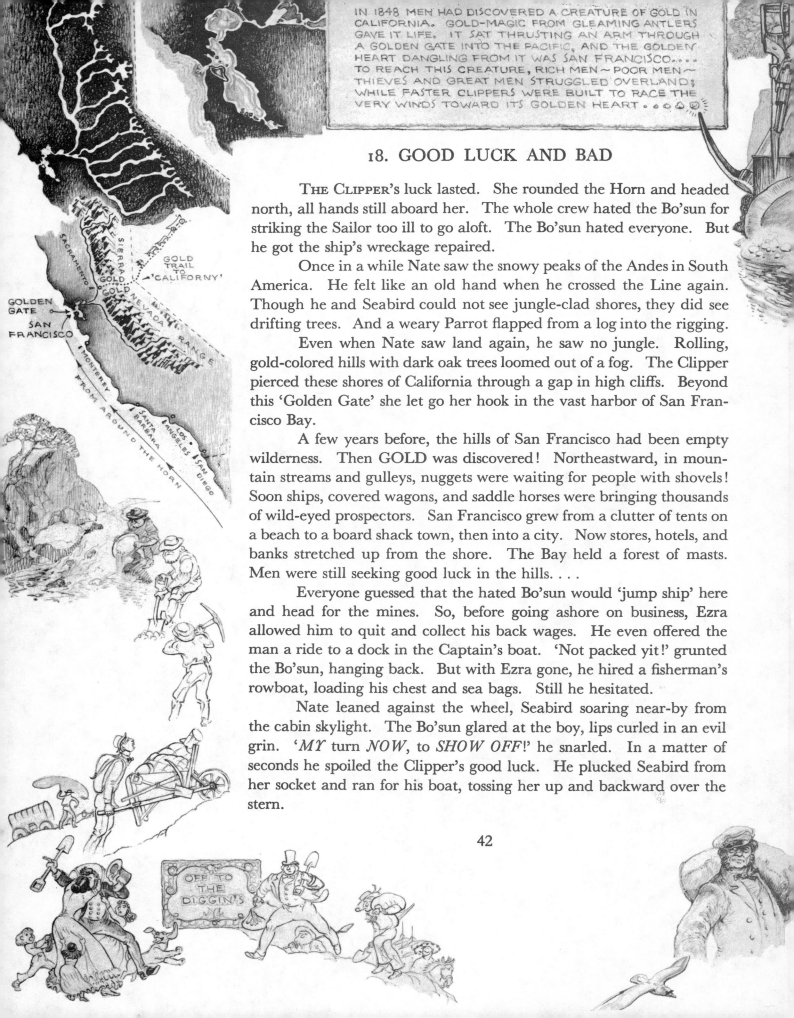

IN 1848 MEN HAD DISCOVERED A CREATURE OF GOLD IN CALIFORNIA. GOLD-MAGIC FROM GLEAMING ANTLERS GAVE IT LIFE. IT SAT THRUSTING AN ARM THROUGH A GOLDEN GATE INTO THE PACIFIC, AND THE GOLDEN HEART DANGLING FROM IT WAS SAN FRANCISCO.... TO REACH THIS CREATURE, RICH MEN ~ POOR MEN ~ THIEVES AND GREAT MEN STRUGGLED OVERLAND; WHILE FASTER CLIPPERS WERE BUILT TO RACE THE VERY WINDS TOWARD ITS GOLDEN HEART.

18. GOOD LUCK AND BAD

THE CLIPPER's luck lasted. She rounded the Horn and headed north, all hands still aboard her. The whole crew hated the Bo'sun for striking the Sailor too ill to go aloft. The Bo'sun hated everyone. But he got the ship's wreckage repaired.

Once in a while Nate saw the snowy peaks of the Andes in South America. He felt like an old hand when he crossed the Line again. Though he and Seabird could not see jungle-clad shores, they did see drifting trees. And a weary Parrot flapped from a log into the rigging.

Even when Nate saw land again, he saw no jungle. Rolling, gold-colored hills with dark oak trees loomed out of a fog. The Clipper pierced these shores of California through a gap in high cliffs. Beyond this 'Golden Gate' she let go her hook in the vast harbor of San Francisco Bay.

A few years before, the hills of San Francisco had been empty wilderness. Then GOLD was discovered! Northeastward, in mountain streams and gulleys, nuggets were waiting for people with shovels! Soon ships, covered wagons, and saddle horses were bringing thousands of wild-eyed prospectors. San Francisco grew from a clutter of tents on a beach to a board shack town, then into a city. Now stores, hotels, and banks stretched up from the shore. The Bay held a forest of masts. Men were still seeking good luck in the hills. . . .

Everyone guessed that the hated Bo'sun would 'jump ship' here and head for the mines. So, before going ashore on business, Ezra allowed him to quit and collect his back wages. He even offered the man a ride to a dock in the Captain's boat. 'Not packed yit!' grunted the Bo'sun, hanging back. But with Ezra gone, he hired a fisherman's rowboat, loading his chest and sea bags. Still he hesitated.

Nate leaned against the wheel, Seabird soaring near-by from the cabin skylight. The Bo'sun glared at the boy, lips curled in an evil grin. '*MY* turn *NOW*, to *SHOW OFF*!' he snarled. In a matter of seconds he spoiled the Clipper's good luck. He plucked Seabird from her socket and ran for his boat, tossing her up and backward over the stern.

42

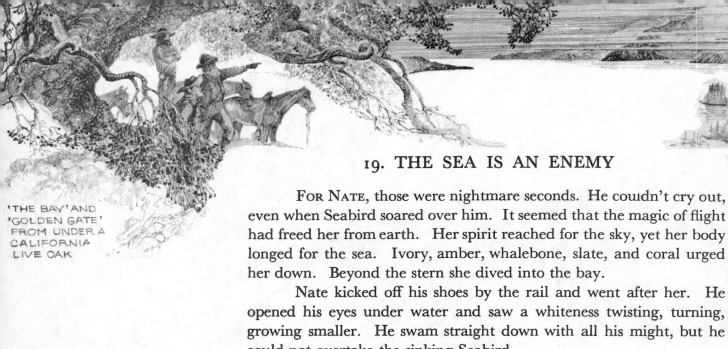

'THE BAY' AND 'GOLDEN GATE' FROM UNDER A CALIFORNIA LIVE OAK

19. THE SEA IS AN ENEMY

FOR NATE, those were nightmare seconds. He couldn't cry out, even when Seabird soared over him. It seemed that the magic of flight had freed her from earth. Her spirit reached for the sky, yet her body longed for the sea. Ivory, amber, whalebone, slate, and coral urged her down. Beyond the stern she dived into the bay.

Nate kicked off his shoes by the rail and went after her. He opened his eyes under water and saw a whiteness twisting, turning, growing smaller. He swam straight down with all his might, but he could not overtake the sinking Seabird.

By now the whole deck knew. 'THAT DIRTY SCUM OF A BO'SUN! HE'S GOT AWAY!'

'FORGET *HIM*!' bawled the Mate. 'GET THAT LAD OUT!'

They hauled the sobbing boy aboard. He slumped on a hatch.

'We're plumb sorry,' said a Cook. 'Seabird was this ship's soul!'

'We just *can't* let ye dive again,' said the Mate. 'Even at this low tide, bottom is fifteen fathoms! No man can live at ninety feet!'

Nate hid from them. 'Let 'im be,' said the Cook. 'Let 'im cry!'

Men wandered miserably to the side, gazing at San Francisco.

'LOOK!' cried somebody. Nate stood on the rail, stripped to the skin. Lifting a short chain in his hands, he leaped. . . .

The chain took him downward now without swimming. Down — through green water, a darker green — and cold! Had he lost track of Seabird about here? He let out air in a bubbly stream. His ears and his lungs hurt. Down, down — and more bubbles, his head pounding. Down — his last air, bubbling away! . . . How good it would feel to let the chain go, and to breathe again! Terror clutched him! Down there — cold depths, crushing! . . . But down there — a dim gray thing — if he could only ——

'He's comin' to, now, Cap'n Ezra,' the Cook was saying. 'But he swallered the whole bay! We sounded for bottom, an' you know what? Fifteen fathoms lie under our *bow*, but only seven *astern*! Nate reached that reef, forty-two feet down! Most grown men wouldn't dare go that deep — but Nate, *he* brought up Seabird!'

44

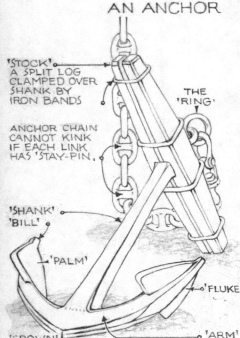

AN ANCHOR

'STOCK'
A SPLIT LOG CLAMPED OVER SHANK BY IRON BANDS

THE 'RING'

ANCHOR CHAIN CANNOT KINK IF EACH LINK HAS 'STAY-PIN'.

'SHANK'
'BILL'

'PALM'

'FLUKE

'CROWN'

'ARM'

ANCHOR SETTLES ON BOTTOM WITH ARMS FLAT, STOCK UPRIGHT. PULL ON CHAIN BY DRIFTING SHIP TOPPLES STOCK, WHILE FLUKE DIGS IN.

1 FATHO
IS 6 FEE

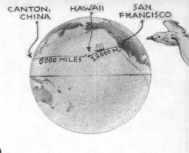
20. THE SEA IS A FRIEND

THUS SEABIRD returned to Nate and Ezra. With them she sailed through the Golden Gate, westbound for the Orient. Day by day Nate finished his nagging tasks swiftly and well, so that he could have more free time with Seabird. Then he would take her aloft to the masthead, where the two of them had a world of sky to themselves. Below, the sun chased rope-shadows over the bulging sails. Far down, the lee rail hissed in foam. Taut rigging sang them its high, wild, joyous songs. And Nate was glad to be alive, riding blue hills of the vast Pacific on flowing wind. . . .

'Aye, the sea is vast and deep,' said Ezra one day, 'in more ways than one. Back home, we think the earth is made of dry land — that the ocean is just a wrinkled old blanket pinned to the beach. 'Tis the other way 'round. The earth is a flooded ball, most of it water. And we, on this sliver of wood adrift for weeks on the deep, have time to think. . . . Nate, I'll confess that when we left home, your actions had me worried. But no more. The sea has taught you well. . . .'

The Clipper anchored at the Sandwich Islands (the native name was 'Hawaii'). Boys and girls swam out to the ship with their parents, wet bodies shining like copper. When Ezra started ashore in his boat, he let Nate swim back with the youngsters. What? This Yankee boy could do their tricks in the water? Then he was one of them! From then on, Nathaniel Brown 'went native.'

They played games in groves of feathery palms, and slid over waterfalls into deep, flower-lined pools. They dived through worlds of waving plants, stiff coral fans, and bright-colored fishes. They raced with surf-boards on the crests of mile-long waves. They ate delicious feasts — meat, seafoods, roots, and fruits baked in hot rock trenches under steaming seaweed. And in the warm evenings scented with ginger blossoms, Nate sprawled on mats in palm-thatched houses and told stories of Seabird, of his father, and far-off New England. . . .

It was all Ezra could do to get Nate back to the ship, headed for China. 'Remember,' he smiled, 'Seabird and I had to leave such islands, too, when we were young. But you'll return.'

46

ON THE VOLCANIC ISLANDS OF HAWAII (HA-WY-EE) NATE SAW FORESTS OF GIANT TREE FERNS.

THIS BUD DROPS ITS SCALES AS IT GROWS DOWNWARD, LEAVING BLOSSOMS TO BECOME BANANAS.

NATE CLIMBED FOR COCONUTS WHICH HE

HUSKED ON A SHARP STAKE, AND CRACKED OPEN ON A ROCK FOR THE SWEET 'MILK' AND WHITE 'MEAT'!

TROPICAL ANGEL F

SMALL FISH, BIG NAME!

HUMUHUMU NUKUNUKU APUAA
(HOO-MOO-HOO-MOO
NOO-KOO-NOO-KOO
AH-POO-AH-AH)

21. MAGIC CAN BE SPUN FROM SIMPLE THINGS

MORE WEEKS swam by on curling hills of water; more weeks of singing rigging and salty spray. Were Nate and Seabird really sailing to the Orient? Or were they hung in a box of billowing cloth while the Orient slid toward them over the sea?

China came first. Nate awoke and knew that China was there. Sun brushed a line of gold hilltops across a misty scroll. Then the roar of a gong tore the mist — and there was China. . . .

And what was China to this boy? It was narrow streets with a serpent's turnings; strings of Shark fins; kites across the sky; teasing smells; tidbits on glowing coals; bales of silk; drums, bells, and jewels; firecrackers popping on poles to frighten devils; packets of tea; and cats, and furry puppies; and glossy Crickets kept for their cheerful songs. . . .

China was white doves wheeling past the red gates of a temple; and incense climbing the shadows to golden dragons. It was two thin men lugging one fat man in his sedan chair; and tottering loads moving past on human feet. . . .

China toiled on barren hills — China slaved on the plains — China swirled on the waters in Sampans and high Junks. But China, big as it was, did not hold all the Orient. The boy saw Siam, Burma, Ceylon, India — and spice-scented islands. . . .

Nate saw men wager on fighting Elephants — and on fishes in a bowl. 'Whole empires,' said Ezra, 'have fought like Elephants (or fishes) — losing, or winning for a time.' Then he and Nate walked in a jungle over ruined cities. 'These cities won great battles,' said Ezra. 'But they destroyed themselves. . . .'

Nate heard wild Cocks crowing. Black Leopards came to drink at a village pool. Pilgrims left food for a stone god asleep in a cave. Cat-sized Bats hung in trees like heavy fruits. A Deer the size of a Rabbit hid under a leaf. A man-eating Tiger coughed in a bamboo thicket. Seabird was almost stolen by jungle Monkeys; she never hinted that, in the Orient, such things had happened to her before. . . .

Even the Clipper seemed new again. In moonlight, her towering sails were ivory pagodas, jeweled with stars. . . .

48

'MOUSE-DEER' 12 INCHES TALL

FRUIT BAT 'FLYING FO WINGSPR UP TO 5 F

22. THE AGE OF SAIL DIES SLOWLY

As YEARS passed, Nate came to know the fabled ports of the world. Ezra taught him the handling of men and ships, and the ways of trade. He could look at a teacup, a live Tiger, or a locomotive, tell the value of each and where it should be placed in a ship's cargo. He became a noted Captain in a new Shipping Company.

Ezra had saved the money he got as a Skipper, added it to the savings of others, and bought the Clipper from her owners. Ezra's Company soon owned shipyards, several Clippers, storehouses, wharves, and a few Steamships.

Long before Ezra was born, the first Steamboats had churned up and down rivers and seacoasts. Later, when old salts argued that it couldn't be done, those banging, belching 'tea-kettles' were crossing oceans! The 'Age of Sail' bloomed in glory with the Clippers. But though for a time they were faster than Steamers, the smoking monsters passed *them* when they were becalmed. Besides, Steamships wasted no precious hours tacking against wind. They plowed a straight furrow, reached port and left again *on time*, scorning any breeze!

The Company's vessel skippered by Nate was a Steamer, but with masts, yards, and sails if the engines broke. When Nate felt happy, he called his ship the 'Half-Way' — half steam, half sail. Seabird, as mascot in his chartroom, sometimes heard him call it other names.

'Thunder! Seabird,' he'd say, 'can't I look at the sky without catching an eyeful of cinders? I *hate* coal smoke! Hang it, Seabird, I'm a man of sail!'

And so, when the wind was headed his way, Nate Brown hooked onto it. 'KILL THE ENGINES!' he'd call. 'SHAKE OUT HER APRONS!' While the grinning Mate would say — 'Sails *do* save coal!' And the Engineer — 'Gives us time to tidy up the machinery!' And sweating Firemen, with their helpers — ''Tis sure wonderful when the Skipper lets us rest, an' leans on the silent wind. . . .'

'Seabird,' Nate would ask, 'and what are *you* saying? Are good ships doomed to wallow in smoke from now to the end of time? Why can't men just fly on the wind — up and into the sky?'

50

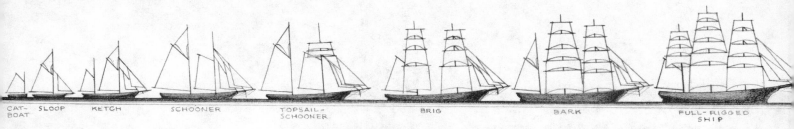

CAT-BOAT   SLOOP   KETCH   SCHOONER   TOPSAIL-SCHOONER   BRIG   BARK   FULL-RIGGED SHIP

23. SOME PEOPLE GROW TO BE MACHINES

NATHANIEL married and had a son. And, just as in the days when Ezra set Seabird above Nate's crib, Seabird now hovered over the cradle of James. The baby's eyes seldom left her, following the swinging dance of her wings.

When Jim was one year old, Grandfather Ezra carved ships for him to sail on puddles. At two, Jim sailed with Seabird and Ezra on catboats. Going-on-three, the baby chatted with Seabird, naming different types of sailing craft in the harbor. But at three years, bright little James Brown lost all interest in sail.

Ezra and Nate took him down to the pounding, hissing engine room of a new Steamer. He stood on the throbbing iron floor, still as a lump of metal. Only his eyes were alive. They followed leaping pistons, jigging crossheads, galloping connecting rods. Then the watching men saw Jim's small body begin to jerk — until fists, elbows, feet, and knees were keeping time to the moving machinery. In his excited dance, with round cheeks puffing, Jim had turned himself into an engine. 'DAD,' yelled Nate, 'THE COMPANY HAS LOST A SAILOR, BUT GAINED AN ENGINEER!'

At six, Jim left Seabird at home when he played in the shipyard shops. At eight he made a metal steam engine model. At ten they fitted him out to sail on the Steamer with his father. However, Nate planned to spend *some* time in running the ship. The boy's questions long since had worn him down. So a young man was hired as a teacher to continue Jim's studies.

From his wide veranda overlooking the bay, Ezra watched the ship's funnel vanish from sight. 'A brainy boy,' he said to himself. 'Aye, he'll be a great credit to the Company some day! But even at ten — I'm afraid he's outgrown Seabird!'

On the steamer, Nate had the same thought. Jim had bolted Seabird to his cabin wall, yet he seemed to ignore her. Nate once said, 'Seabird helped me to know the sea. Are you glad she's yours? Aren't you glad Grandfather carved her?'

'Of course!' said Jim. 'You *know* I admire odd inventions!'

52

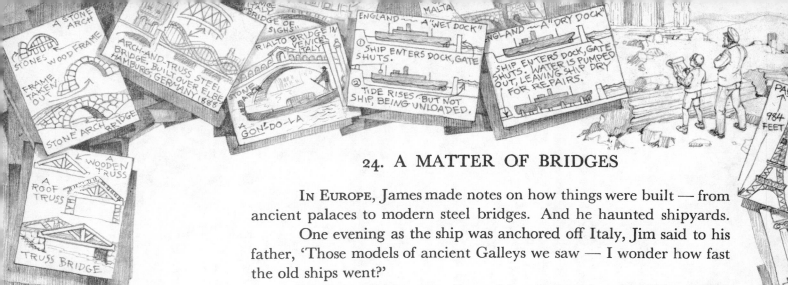

24. A MATTER OF BRIDGES

IN EUROPE, James made notes on how things were built — from ancient palaces to modern steel bridges. And he haunted shipyards.

One evening as the ship was anchored off Italy, Jim said to his father, 'Those models of ancient Galleys we saw — I wonder how fast the old ships went?'

'As fast as aching muscles could send them,' replied Nate. 'This Mediterranean Sea is a nest where ships were hatched. Egyptians built some of the first. Their boats were copied by others, until even our steel ship holds many of the ancient inventions. One thing, though, we *have* changed. We use steam. In the old days, when wind wasn't right, slaves rowed Galleys to drum-beats. Bull-whips cracked on the bare flesh of men chained to oars. Thunder! Jim, you talk about building such things as bridges! War and Trade have always traveled on bridges of sweating human backs!'

Jim was twelve when he saw his Grandfather again. 'Did you learn things?' asked Ezra. 'Think you'll rebuild the Company's ships?'

'Maybe some day, Sir,' Jim replied solemnly. 'And — yes, Sir, I learned things. Father and I had a little talk — off Italy, it was. I got to wondering about all the slaves and common Sailors who had worked on ships. One evening I looked at Seabird and thought, "You saw Grandfather slaving on the Whaler. You saw Father slave as a Clipper's Cabin Boy. Do Sailors work hard today?"

'To find out, I worked with Deck Hands, Coal Passers, Firemen, Oilers. In a month I could say to Seabird, "Men work hard today, even on a Steamer!"'

'So!' said Ezra, leaning back and staring at Jim. 'An' what did you decide?'

'Well, I decided that some day I'd build engines running on oil, not coal. Firemen and helpers won't shovel, they'll just turn valves. And I'll plan ships so Sailors can have better cabins, better food, and more pay for what they do!...'

'Strange talk,' said Ezra, 'from a boy! And I thought you'd outgrown Seabird!'

54

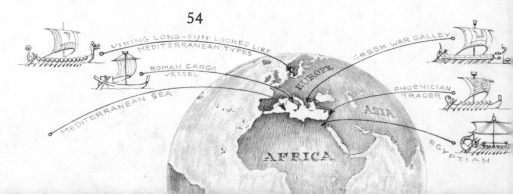

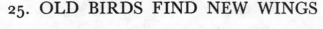

25. OLD BIRDS FIND NEW WINGS

When James Brown became a man, he was known not as a great Sea Captain, but as a great ship designer. His last vessel, now being riveted together with chattering hammers in the yards, would be run by steam engines burning oil. No coal would roar into bunkers. No men in hot, black caverns would shovel like mad. "'Twould take a big parade of Whales and months of back-breakin' toil to fill those,' laughed Ezra, pointing his cane at the huge petroleum tanks. And Nate laughed with him. 'Imagine! Firemen merely turning shiny valves! No coal smoke! No cinders in the eye!' And James said quietly, 'Better cabins for Sailors — good beds, better food and wages!'

Jim's son was born months before this ship was launched. Kenneth, they named him — Ken for short. Newspapers made much of the fact that Ken, the fourth generation of this famous family, had been born a full century after Ezra's birth. The papers ran in big type, 'AND THE GREAT–GRANDFATHER STILL LIVING!'

Ezra in his crowded office corner read this and smiled. 'You *BET* he's living!' he said. 'And he's goin' to celebrate! In a plane! Ever since I saw that Ivory Gull, I've hankered ——'

'*You're* going to fly?' cried Nate. 'At a hundred? I always promised Seabird that *I'd* fly! . . . I'm going with you!'

'At *seventy-three*?' said James. 'Now I'm thirty-seven, but ——'

The newspapers ran extras, with huge photographs. Great-Grandfather, Grandfather, and Father of the newborn heir of the great Shipping Company had all flown in planes! Three — no, *four* of the Company! Ezra had held Seabird! . . .

On the day the new Oil Burner was launched, Seabird was hung above Ken's cradle. The glistening ship made the ancient sea seem new. And in much the same way, Seabird was made young again. Time after time she had started to grow older with her last companion. But before she could grow too old, new eyes regarded her with wonder. At that instant, her youthful magic was renewed. Once more the old world became a fresh new place for living. In this way, Seabird could never grow really old!

56

MAIN DINING ROOM

A SWIMMING POOL

26. THREE PARTNERS INSPECT A NEW SHIP

IN THE family car they worried about Ezra and drafts.

'I *could* die from a draft,' grunted the old man, 'but the good Lord laid my keel uncommon tough. A hundred and five years He's let me drift around, puffin' wind at me —— How old are *you*, Ken? Yep, all of five years! . . . Ken boy, where we headin'?'

'To visit Daddy's newest Liner, Cap'n Ezra! And we're *here*!'

'Great sawfish — that a ship? Thought 'twas a warehouse! Now, set me in the wheelchair — Ken, you an' Seabird stick close!'

An hour later, these three 'partners' rested on deck. 'Tired, Cap'n?' asked the small boy. 'Have we let you see too much?'

'A trifle tired. . . . This vessel, it's — it's too *big*! Elevators for up an' down! Banquet halls! Did I see *palm trees* growin' on a deck?'

'Yes, sir, in marble boxes! And you saw swimming pools, and shops with candy and toys. . . . You *do* think she's a beautiful ship — don't you, Cap'n Ezra?'

'Aye, boy — a thing of beauty — and excitement. . . . Old ships go an' new ships come, bigger an' better. This floatin' city now — at least she's *bigger*! But *why?* Just so restless tourists can eat too much, dance all night aboard, an' *say* they've seen the world! But they'll be too busy gossipin' to even look at India!'

'Oh, *I'll* look at India, Sir!' said Ken quickly. 'When Seabird and I sail with Daddy we'll look *very* 'specially at India!'

'Aye, you'll *see* things!' chuckled Ezra. 'Right now — see that plane yonder? *There's* a ship of the future. All of us who have had Seabird have longed to fly. Some day, Ken, you'll ride in great ships across the sky. Take care that you never forget the first feeling of awe and wonder at flying through space. . . .

'People are puzzled why I feel young, at five years beyond a century. Maybe it started in the freedom I felt, one day at a masthead. I felt that I was lifted upward, floating in the sky! . . . Folks say 'twas only a Gull I saw there in the snowstorm. Aye, but somehow its magic got bottled up in Seabird. And long after I am gone, she will still be shaping people and things. She'll still be soaring. . . .'

58